NS

Series Editor: Rosalind Kerven

Heinemann Educational Publishers,
Halley Court, Jordan Hill, Oxford OX2 8EJ
a division of Reed Educational & Professional Publishing Ltd.

MELBOURNE AUCKLAND
FLORENCE PRAGUE MADRID ATHENS
SINGAPORE TOKYO SAOPAULO
CHICAGO PORTSMOUTH (NH) MEXICO
IBADAN GABORONE JOHANNESBURG
KAMPALA NAIROBI

© Heinemann Educational 1995

First published 1995

03 02 01 00
10 9 8 7 6 5 4 3

The right of the author to be identified as the author of the work has been asserted.

British Library Cataloguing in Publication Data
A catalogue record for this book is available from the British Library

Starter Pack
1 of each of 12 titles: ISBN 0 435 00957 5

Library Hardback
Beowulf and the Dragon: ISBN 0 431 06507 1
Pack 1 – 1 each of 6 titles: ISBN 0 431 06498 9
Pack 2 – 1 each of 6 titles: ISBN 0 431 06499 7

Typeset by Sue Vaudin
Printed in Hong Kong

Acknowledgements
Title page and border illustration, pp 2/3: Nadine Wickendon;
map, p2: Dave Bowyer; photographs, p3 (top, bottom left): Michael Holford;
(bottom right): C M Dixon

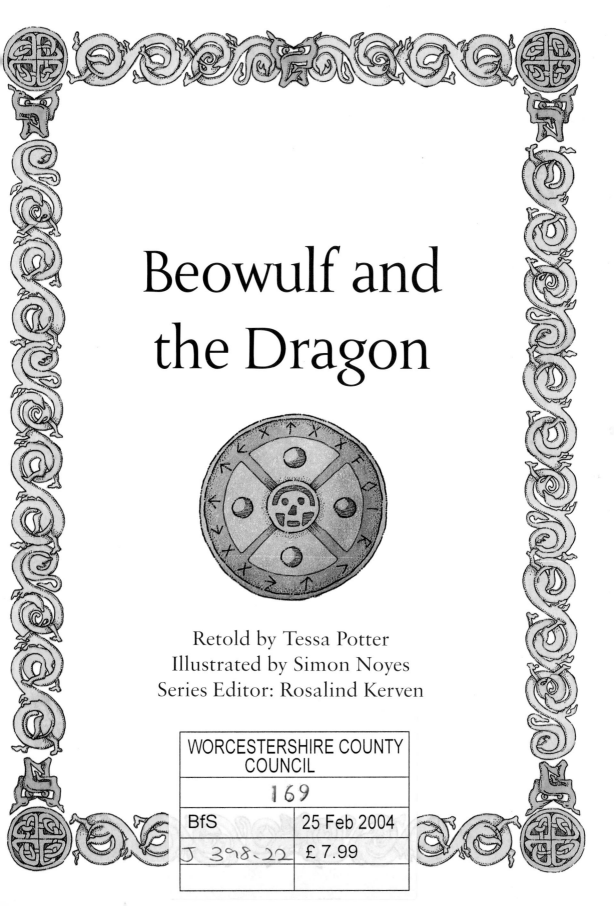

Beowulf and
the Dragon

Retold by Tessa Potter
Illustrated by Simon Noyes
Series Editor: Rosalind Kerven

Introduction

'Beowulf' is an Anglo-Saxon poem.
It was probably written in England
about 1,200 years ago.
Invaders and settlers from other
countries brought the story to
England.
The story takes place in the Land
of the Geats, in what is now
Sweden.

Map of Anglo-Saxon England

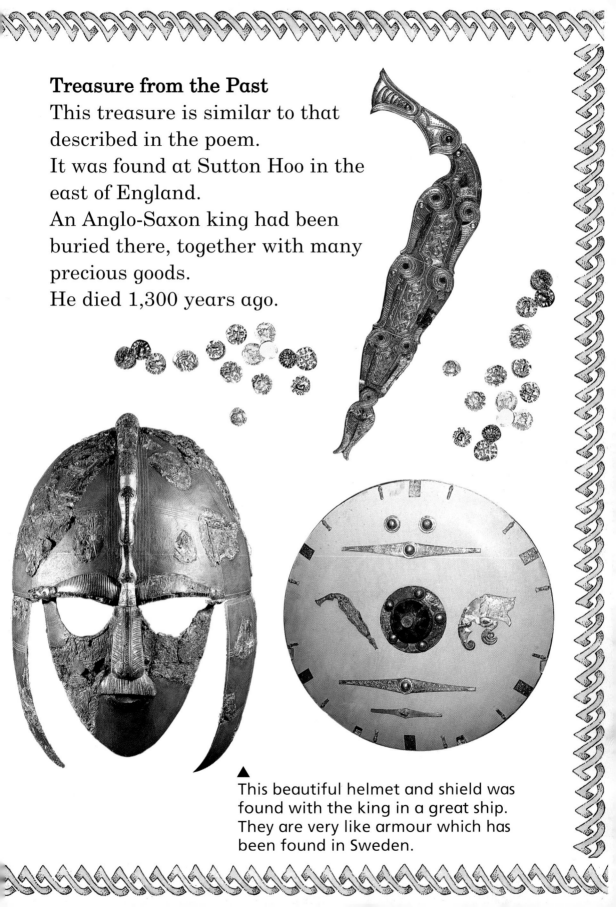

Treasure from the Past

This treasure is similar to that described in the poem.

It was found at Sutton Hoo in the east of England.

An Anglo-Saxon king had been buried there, together with many precious goods.

He died 1,300 years ago.

▲
This beautiful helmet and shield was found with the king in a great ship. They are very like armour which has been found in Sweden.

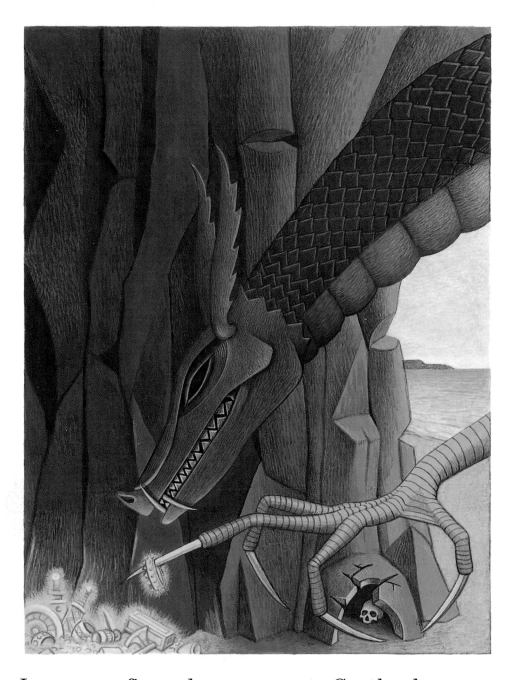

Long ago a fierce dragon came to Geatland.
The dragon made its home in a dark cave at
the edge of the sea.
Inside that cave the dragon found a hoard of
golden treasure and fine weapons.

4

The dragon stood guard over the hoard.
He coiled his body around the treasure.
The dragon grew bigger and bigger until only
a tiny glimmer of gold could be seen.
No-one came near the cave for
three hundred years.

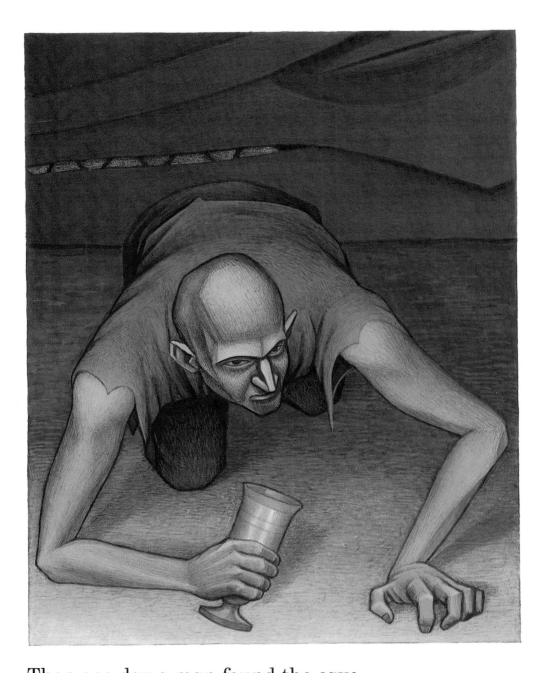

Then one day a man found the cave.
He crept inside.
He saw a glimmer of gold under the dragon.
While the dragon slept,
the man stole a golden cup.

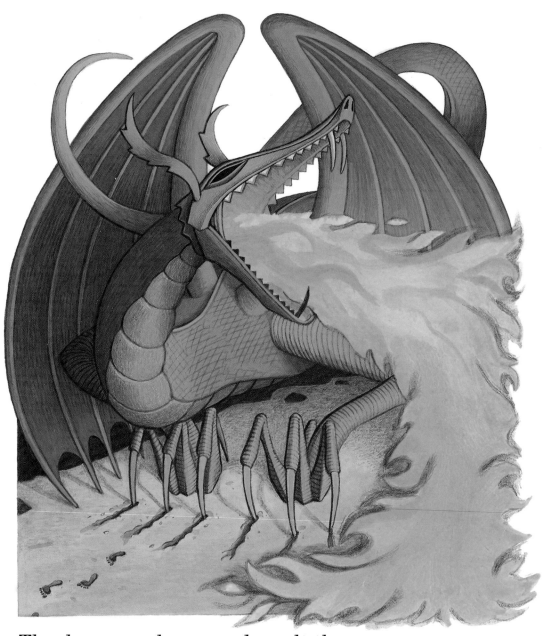

The dragon woke up and smelt the man.
He saw footprints in the sand and
found that a piece of the treasure was missing.
He knew that his gold would never be safe again.
The dragon roared a great roar.
He spat fire and smoke in his fury.

That night the dragon flew out over
Geatland looking for the thief.
He burnt down houses and villages.
He burnt down trees and fields.
His anger was terrible.
Wherever he flew his hot breath
spread flames over the ground.

People ran for their lives,
but no-one could escape the dragon's fire.
Every night he left his cave and flew over the land,
burning everything he saw.
Even the king's great hall was burnt to the ground.

The king's name was Beowulf.
He had ruled Geatland for fifty years.
He had won many battles and destroyed
terrible monsters.
He was old now, but he knew
he had one last battle to fight.
He must kill this dragon and save his people.

King Beowulf took a great shield of iron.
Only iron could protect him from the flames.
He chose eleven of his most brave soldiers
to ride with him.
One of these was his young relative, Wiglaf.

The man who had stolen the dragon's treasure
led the way to the dragon's cave.
They followed a terrible trail
of black fields and burnt forests.
At last they came to a high cliff.
The man pointed to a cave in the rocks below.
Steam and smoke rose up from the ground.

King Beowulf took his sword and his shield
and ran down to the rocks.
He cried out in a loud voice,
"Come out evil one, killer-by-night.
I have come to destroy you and win the gold.
You will no longer bring death to my people."

The dragon heard Beowulf and flew out.
The great beast stood on the sand,
hissing and lashing his tail.
The scales on his back glowed red and golden.
Flames poured from his mouth.
The ground shook.

King Beowulf was not afraid.
He moved closer holding his shield high.
He lifted his sword and struck the dragon hard.
The dragon screamed and spat more fire.
The fire wrapped Beowulf in a ball of flames.
Even the iron shield began to melt...

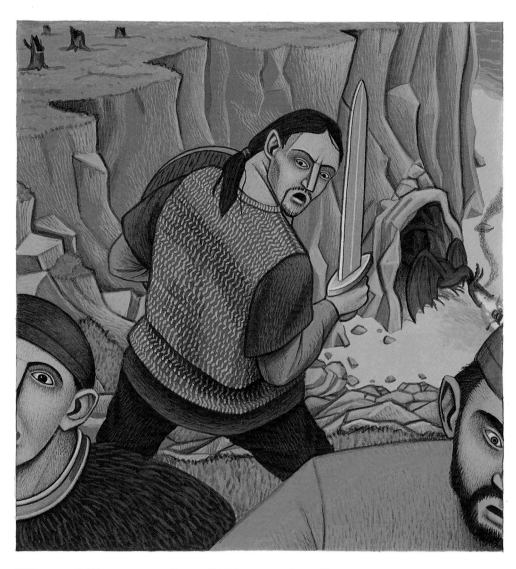

The soldiers on the cliff saw the flames
around Beowulf and began to run away.
Wiglaf called after them, "How can you leave
our king when he needs us most?
Has he not given us gold and fine weapons?
Did we not promise to be brave and loyal and
to help him always?"
But the soldiers were afraid of the dragon.

Only Wiglaf ran down to help the king.
His wooden shield burst into flames as he got near,
but he did not turn back.
The old king found new strength
with young Wiglaf at his side.
He lifted his sword again to kill the dragon.
But this time the sword broke ...

The dragon lifted its great claws and
tore at Beowulf wounding him terribly.
At that moment Wiglaf crept under the beast
and struck the dragon from below.
The dragon's blood spilled on to the ground
and the fierce flames died down.

Now, with his last strength, King Beowulf took his
knife and cut the beast in two.
Then he staggered to the rocks.
His life was nearly over, but the dragon was dead
and his people were saved.

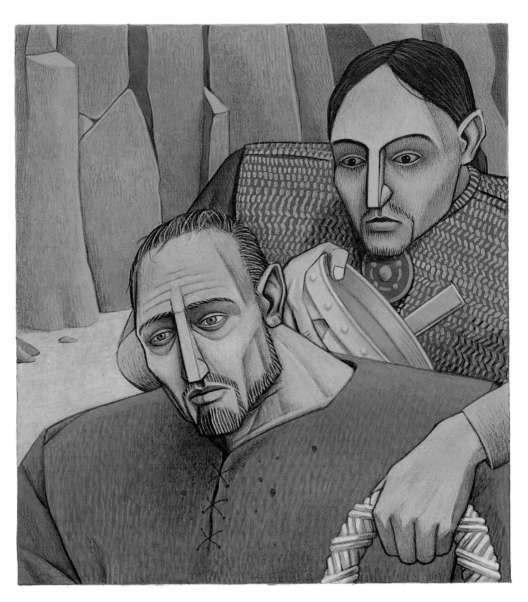

Wiglaf ran to his king's side.

"I am dying," said Beowulf.

"Take my helmet and battle armour, brave Wiglaf.

And take this golden collar.

I have no son of my own,

so you shall be the next King of the Geats.

Now, before I die let me see the dragon's gold."

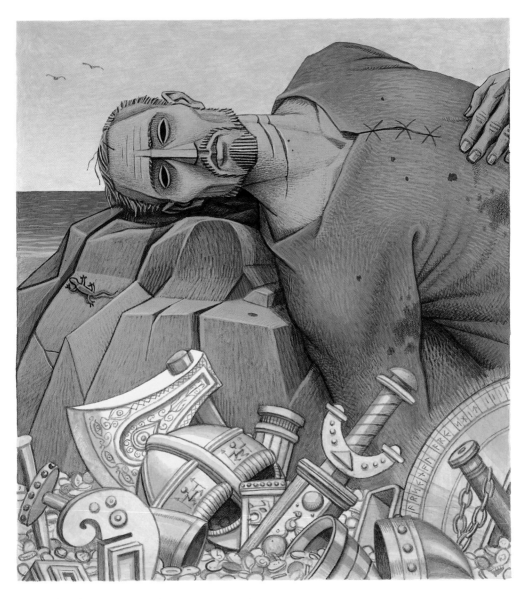

Wiglaf ran to the dragon's cave.
He brought out all the treasure he could carry
and laid it on the rocks.
Golden cups and rings, swords and helmets,
gleaming and glistening in the sunlight.
The great king gazed at them,
and then he died.

They carried King Beowulf's body to the cliff top.
Around him they hung shields and weapons
from the dragon's hoard.
They made ready a great funeral fire.
The torch was lit.
For many miles around,
the people of Geatland saw the funeral fire
and knew that their good king was dead.

Then Wiglaf ordered that a high stone mound
be built around the ashes of their king.
And in the barrow they laid the dragon's gold.
"Our noble king lost his life to
win this gold," said Wiglaf.
"Let it return with him to the darkness."

And so Beowulf's Barrow was made,
a great mound of stones high on the cliff top.
The stones shone white in the sun.
All those who sailed on the sea below
looked up and remembered Beowulf.
Beowulf the gold giver, Beowulf the great soldier,
Beowulf the dragon killer.